Penguins of Antarctica

Sally Cowan

Contents

Antarctic Penguins

Penguins are seabirds. Most penguins live in the **Southern Hemisphere**.

Emperor penguins and Adelie (say: *A-dell-ee*) penguins live in **Antarctica**. Some other kinds of penguins live on the islands nearby.

Although penguins are birds, they cannot fly. But they are excellent swimmers. Their **sleek** bodies, strong flippers and webbed feet allow them to glide through the water. They can also dive very deep in search of food.

Antarctica is the land around the South Pole.

emperor penguins

Adelie penguin

Living in the Cold

Penguins have a thick layer of **blubber** on their bodies. It keeps them warm on the ice and in the cold water.

Emperor penguins are the largest penguins, and have the most blubber. They grow more than a metre tall and can weigh up to 40 kilograms.

Penguins have black feathers on their backs and white feathers on their bellies. Some kinds of penguins also have coloured feathers around their heads. Penguins' feathers completely cover their skin, and protect them from cold water and wind.

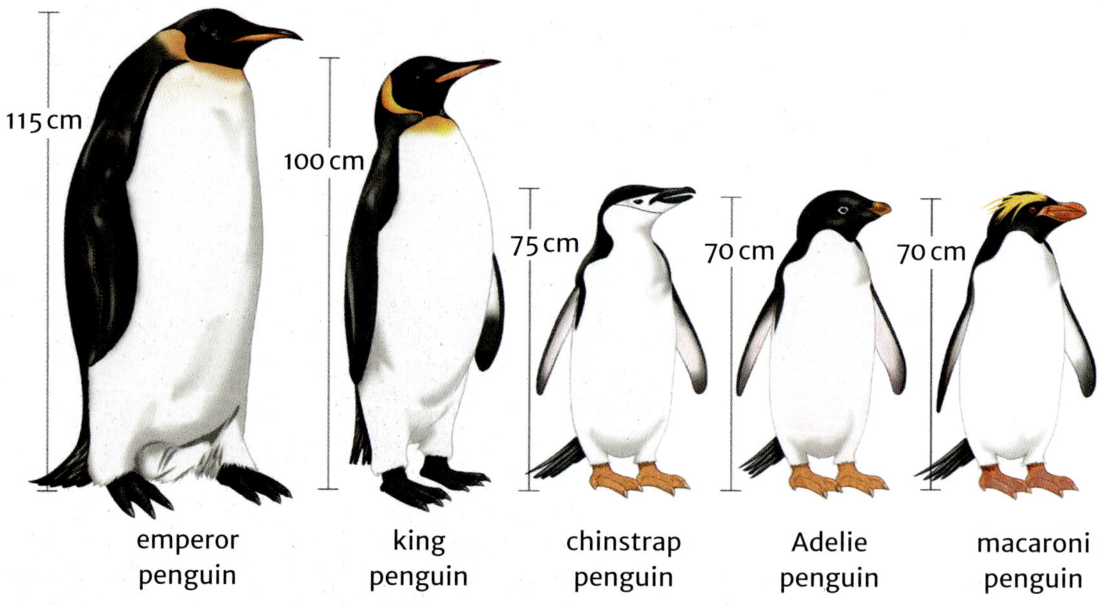

This chart shows the heights of Antarctic penguins.

Macaroni penguins have brightly coloured feathers on their heads.

Emperor penguins are the largest and tallest penguins.

Penguins often have to walk on slippery ice. They walk upright on their short, stocky legs, following each other in a long line. They do not look very **agile** as they waddle and hop on the ice, but they can move quite fast. They also slide along the ice on their bellies.

Emperor penguins walk and slide along the ice.

Penguins use their strong claws to climb up steep ice cliffs and over rocks.

An Adelie penguin walks over rocks.

An Icy Home

The penguins of Antarctica live in one of the harshest **habitats** on Earth. Antarctica is at the South Pole. It is the coldest, driest and windiest place in the world. Most of the land is always covered in ice. Ice also covers large areas of the Southern Ocean.

In winter, the sky stays dark, it snows and there are fierce **blizzards**.

In summer, it is light for most of the day. Much of the sea ice melts, and some areas of the coast have no snow or ice.

In winter there are blizzards.

It is not as cold in summer.

Penguins find their food in the ocean. They hunt fish, squid and **krill**.

Seals, orcas and other whales also live in the ocean. The penguins' main predators are seals and orcas.

Adelie penguins do not go into the water when they can see orcas.

Antarctica is called a "cold desert" because it does not rain very much.

Diving for Prey

Penguins dive to catch their prey underwater. Adelie penguins can dive as deep as 175 metres. Emperor penguins can dive even deeper, to more than 500 metres. Both kinds of penguins usually stay underwater for about 6 minutes. However, emperor penguins can stay underwater for more than 20 minutes.

tiny krill under the ice

Emperor penguins hunt krill underwater.

Penguins often hunt in groups. They can round up more fish and krill when they hunt together. They catch prey in their sharp beaks and swallow it underwater.

Penguins come up to the surface to breathe and rest. Then they take a deep breath and dive again.

A group of Adelie penguins dive into the water.

Caring for Chicks

Antarctic penguins spend a lot of time out of the water in **colonies**. This is where they **breed**, and care for their chicks. They search for the same **mate** every year, calling loudly to each other.

Emperor Penguins

Before winter, emperor penguins walk long distances from the sea to their colonies to breed.
If young penguins have not bred before, they find a mate.

Each female emperor penguin lays one egg.
She quickly moves the egg onto her mate's feet, being careful to keep it off the cold ice.
The male then covers the egg with a fold of fat, to keep it warm.

The female returns to the sea to hunt for food for the next three months.

Emperor penguins are the only animals that breed during the winter in Antarctica.

A father emperor penguin cares for an egg.

The male emperor penguins care for their eggs for the whole winter, without eating. During blizzards, they huddle together in a large group. The penguins slowly move from the cold outer edges of the group to the middle, where it is warm.

Male emperor penguins huddle together all winter, caring for their eggs.

When the females return from the sea, the males have lost half their body weight. The eggs have usually hatched by this time. The females bring up food from their stomachs to feed their small fluffy chicks.

The hungry males return to the sea to feed. But they come back soon to help feed their chicks.

When the chicks have grown black and white feathers, they are ready to swim and hunt for themselves.

A mother emperor penguin feeds a chick.

Older chicks lose their fluffy feathers and grow black and white feathers instead.

Adelie Penguins

Adelie penguins breed after the harsh winter. They gather on the shores of Antarctica. The males build nests of pebbles on dry ground.

Female Adelie penguins usually lay two eggs. The penguin parents take turns looking after the eggs. One parent is always there to protect the eggs from birds that would eat them. The other parent hunts for food.

After the eggs hatch, both parents keep on caring for the tiny chicks.

An Adelie penguin cares for two chicks.

When the chicks are bigger, the parents go hunting and leave the chicks on the shore. The chicks gather together to keep warm while their parents are away.

When the chicks are nine weeks old, they leave the colony and hunt for themselves.

Penguins can recognise the calls of their own chicks in colonies with thousands of penguins.

Older chicks stay together while all their parents go hunting.

Penguins of the Antarctic Islands

Other kinds of penguins, such as macaroni, chinstrap and king penguins, live on the islands near Antarctica.

Macaroni penguins have black faces, and scruffy yellow feathers on their heads.

Chinstrap penguins have a narrow band of black feathers under their white chins.

King penguins have bright orange patches on their ears and chests.

macaroni penguins

chinstrap penguins

king penguins

The Future for Antarctic Penguins

The **climate** of Earth is getting warmer.
It is changing the habitats of Antarctic penguins.

Warmer seas are melting the sea ice more quickly than usual. Krill are an important food for penguins, but the krill need sea ice to survive. Krill eat **algae** that grows under the sea ice, and the ice also gives them shelter from rough seas.

Krill eat algae under the sea ice.

If there is less sea ice, there will be less krill in the water. Penguins already compete for krill with seals and whales. It might become even harder for penguins to find enough to eat.

People catch large amounts of krill. Krill are used to make health foods.

Adelie penguins dive into the water to hunt.

Antarctica is usually cold and dry, but if the climate continues to warm, penguin habitats could become more rainy and wet. Penguin eggs and chicks cannot survive in puddles of water.

Some penguins might move to drier parts of Antarctica to raise their chicks. They might also find different foods to eat. These special creatures are good at surviving in the harshest conditions.

Glossary

agile (*adjective*) able to move quickly and easily

algae (*noun*) a kind of tiny plant that grows in water

Antarctica (*proper noun*) the huge area of land around the South Pole

blizzards (*noun*) cold winter snowstorms

blubber (*noun*) a layer of fat under the skin of marine mammals

breed (*verb*) to produce young

climate (*noun*) the weather patterns throughout the year

colonies (*noun*) large groups of animals that gather together on land

habitats (*noun*) places where animals usually live

krill (*noun*) tiny animals with shells that live in the sea

mate (*noun*) one of a pair of animals that breed and care for babies together

sleek (*adjective*) smoothly shaped for fast movement

Southern Hemisphere (*proper noun*) the half of Earth that is south of the equator, which is the imaginary line around the middle of Earth

Index